Top 10 Playmakers

Chris W. Sehnert

ABDO & Daughters
Publishing

Published by Abdo & Daughters, 4940 Viking Drive, Suite 622, Edina, Minnesota 55435.

Printed in the United States.

Cover and Interior Photo credits: Wide World Photos
Bettmann Archives
Allsports
Sports Illustrated

Edited by Paul Joseph

Library of Congress Cataloging-In-Publication Data

Sehnert, Chris W.
    Top 10 playmakers / Chris W. Sehnert.
    p. cm.
    summary: Profiles ten great NBA guards, including Larry Bird, Bob Cousy, Walt Frazier, Jerry West, and Magic Johnson.
    ISBN 1-56239-796-6
    1. Guards (Basketball)--United States--Biography--Juvenile literature. 2. Guards (Basketball)--Rating of--United States--Juvenile literature. 3. Basketball--Offense--Juvenile literature. (1. Basketball players.) I. Title. II. Series: Sehnert, Chris W. top 10 champions.
    GV884.A1S456 1997
    796.323'64'092273--dc21
    (B)   97-20093
                                               CIP
                                               AC

Table of Contents

Bob Cousy 4

Oscar Robertson 8

Jerry West 12

John Havlicek 16

Walt Frazier 20

Julius Erving 24

Larry Bird 28

Magic Johnson 32

Isiah Thomas.. 36

Michael Jordan.................................... 40

Glossary.. 44

Index 46

Bob Cousy

Basketball is a colorful game. The fundamental skills required to play include dribbling, passing, and shooting. Beyond the basics are a number of unique strategies such as the "Give-and-Go," the "Alley-Oop," the "High-Low-Post," and "Back-Door-Screen." The great players of the National Basketball Association (NBA) are masters of executing these and other techniques. Often, their athletic artistry seems to surpass the capabilities of mortal man, and they are given nicknames to reflect such wizardry. Before there was "Air," there was "Magic." And prior to "Hondo the Magnificent," came the "Houdini of the Hardwood!"

Bob Cousy was the Boston Celtics point-guard for 13 seasons. He was an NBA All-Star in every one of those years, and the Celtics were the NBA Champions six times. The point-guard is the predominate *playmaker* on a basketball team. They are in charge of bringing the ball up-court, setting-up the offensive play, and getting the ball to the person with the best opportunity to score. In the case of the fast-breaking Boston Celtics, this often occurred at top-speed.

Robert Joseph Cousy was born in the Yorkville section of New York City, New York. His mother, Julliette, was also a New York native, but had moved to France at the age of four. Bob's father, Joseph, was from Alsace-Lorraine, France. He brought his wife back to New York, where he became a cab driver just six-months before the birth of their son. Bob grew up speaking French, in a German neighborhood. Before long, he became obsessed with the American sport of basketball. Bob's family moved to St. Albans,

New York, when he was 11 years old. His childhood memories include playing stickball in the streets and swimming in the East River. Prior to gaining status as "Houdini of the Hardwood," he built a reputation on the neighborhood pavement. "He never even went to the movies," a neighbor recalls. "I never saw a person as crazy about anything as he was about basketball."

After graduating from Andrew Jackson High School, Bob attended the College of the Holy Cross in Worcester, Massachusetts. He had been named the captain of New York City's All-Scholastic Five as a high school senior. As a sophomore at Holy Cross his team won the National Championship of college basketball. Bob was the nations All-American point-guard as a senior, and he graduated with a degree in Business Administration.

In 1950, the NBA was beginning its fifth season of play. Bob Cousy joined the Boston Celtics that season, and was soon recognized as the league's top *playmaker*. His highly developed ball-handling skills set the standard for point-guards to come. His passes came from all directions, and seemed to be sent with radar. Whether launched, lobbed, or bounced, they rarely missed their mark. Beginning in 1953, Bob led the NBA in assists eight straight times, and he remains as Boston's all-time leader in the category.

When Bill Russell became the Celtics' center in 1956, the team began a string of championship seasons. Bob was the NBA's Most Valuable Player (MVP) that season, with a scoring average of over 20 points per game. Bob Cousy, Basketball's original magician, retired in 1963. He was inducted into the Naismith Memorial Basketball Hall-of-Fame in 1970.

PROFILE:
Bob Cousy
Born: August 9, 1928
Height: 6' 1"
Weight: 175 pounds
Position: Guard
College: Holy Cross University
Teams: Boston Celtics (1950-1963), Cincinnati Royals (1969-1970)

CHAMPIONSHIP

SEASONS

1956-57
NBA Championship
Boston Celtics (4) vs. St. Louis Hawks (3)

1958-59
NBA Championship
Boston Celtics (4) vs. Minneapolis Lakers (0)

1959-60
NBA Championship
Boston Celtics (4) vs. St. Louis Hawks (3)

1960-61
NBA Championship
Boston Celtics (4) vs. St. Louis Hawks (1)

1961-62
NBA Championship
Boston Celtics (4) vs. Los Angeles Lakers (3)

1962-63
NBA Championship
Boston Celtics (4) vs. Los Angeles Lakers (2)

LUCK OF THE DRAW

Because of Bob Cousy's relatively small size, a career in professional basketball was less than a certainty. Bob was chosen by the Tri-Cities Blackhawks (the original Atlanta Hawks) in the 1950 NBA Draft. He was then traded to the Chicago Stags, who dropped out of the league before the season began.

The names of the players from the defunct Stags organization were placed in a hat for the remaining NBA teams to pick from. The Boston Celtics drew first and pulled Bob Cousy out of the hat. It was a fitting way to kickoff the career of a basketball wizard.

Bob Cousy playing for Holy Cross College.

COACH COOZ

Bob Cousy was just 35 years old when he retired from professional basketball. He had grown tired of the NBA's rigorous schedule, which kept him from his wife and daughters. The next season he began an 11 year career as a head-coach. He guided Boston College to five post-season tournament appearances in his six years there.

Cousy playing with the Celtics.

The Celtics' legendary coach, Red Auerbach, had figured "Cooz" would be his eventual replacement. Bob's unexpected retirement, however, meant the job would go to teammate Bill Russell. In 1969, Bob left Boston College to become the head coach for the NBA's Cincinnati Royals (the original Sacramento Kings). Cincinnati's star player was Oscar Robertson. Bob occasionally inserted himself into the lineup that season, giving the Royals two of the greatest point-guards to ever play the game!

HARDWOOD HERO

Bob's experience as a French-speaking boy growing up in New York's 'German-town' left a lasting impression on him. Being well aware of the treatment minorities often receive, he wrote a paper for a class at Holy Cross entitled "The Persecution of Minority Groups."

As a rookie with the Boston Celtics, Bob was joined by Charles Cooper, the first African-American to play on an NBA team. After an exhibition game in Raleigh, North Carolina, Cooper was not allowed to stay in the team's hotel. When he was granted permission to take a train back home, Bob insisted on accompanying him. Their friendship made a difficult situation a little easier.

Bob Cousy retiring from the Celtics.

Robertson

Playmakers have a specific role on a basketball team. Like a quarterback in football they must understand the defensive alignment and distribute the ball. By drawing attention to themselves, they may free-up a teammate for an open shot. If the defense holds its ground, the *playmaker* must create a shot of their own. In short, they must be able to do it all.

One player who fits this description to the letter was known as "Big O." After completing perhaps the greatest college basketball career in history, Oscar Robertson spent 14 seasons in the NBA. In the 1960s, Oscar frequently led the league in assists, always led his team in scoring, and was once among the league leaders in rebounds. Then in 1970, he joined another one of college basketball's all-time greats to bring the Milwaukee Bucks an NBA Championship.

Oscar Palmer Robertson was born near Charlotte, Tennessee. He was the youngest of Mrs. Mazell Bell Robertson's three sons. The family lived in a rundown shack owned by Mazell's father, Early Bell, until

Oscar was three years old. Next, they moved to a west-side ghetto in Indianapolis, Indiana. It was there that the Robertson boys took up basketball. Oscar's oldest brother, Bailey, nailed a peach basket to the back of their tar paper roofed house and used anything suitable for a ball.

When Oscar was 11 years old, his parents were divorced. His mother went to work as a housekeeper for a family on the wealthy side of town. Upon watching her employer's son discard an old basketball, she promptly dug it out of the garbage, brought it home, and presented it to her own youngest son. "He was always bouncing it," Mazell remembers. "He'd bring it to the dinner table and he took it to bed with him. When the sound of the bumping stopped, we knew that Oscar was ready to go to sleep."

Oscar attended Crispus Attucks High School, where his unprecedented skills soon became apparent. He led his team to the first undefeated season in the rich history of Indiana high school basketball. The perfect season was part of a 45-game winning streak that included two straight State High School Championships. In addition to setting several scoring records on the basketball court, Oscar was a brilliant pitcher for the baseball team, set a high school record for the high-jump, and graduated near the top of his class as a member of the National Honor Society.

After receiving several scholarship offers from colleges across the country, Oscar chose to attend the University of Cincinnati. There, he was named the College Player of the Year in each of his three seasons of varsity eligibility. He set a single-game scoring record (56) in his sophomore season, and graduated as the highest scoring player in college basketball history.

Oscar remained in Cincinnati through the first 10 seasons of his professional career. He was the NBA's Rookie of the Year in 1961, and the league's MVP three years later. The Royals, meanwhile, rose from near bankruptcy into a respectable force. In the 1960s, however, the NBA title regularly resided in Boston.

The Milwaukee Bucks were a third-year expansion team when they traded for Big O in 1970. Their leader was a second-year player who had carried UCLA to three straight National College Basketball Championships, before becoming the 1970 NBA Rookie of the Year. Oscar Robertson and Kareem Abdul-Jabbar combined to bring Milwaukee their first and only NBA Championship in their first season together.

Oscar Robertson's career ended in 1974. He currently ranks fifth on the all-time list of scorers and third on the all-time list for assists. A *playmaker* who could do it all, Big O was inducted into the Naismith Memorial Hall-of-Fame in 1979.

PROFILE:
Oscar Robertson
Born: November 24, 1938
Height: 6' 5"
Weight: 220 pounds
Position: Guard
College: University of Cincinnati
Teams: Cincinnati Royals (1960-1970), Milwaukee Bucks (1970-1974)

CHAMPIONSHIP

SEASONS

Oscar Robertson going in for a layup.

1970-71

NBA Championship
Milwaukee Bucks (4) vs.
Baltimore Bullets (0)

HUMBLE BEGINNINGS

Oscar's oldest brother Bailey was also a star basketball player at Crispus Attucks High School. He attended Indiana Central College where he broke the career scoring record for Indiana colleges, and later played for the Harlem Globetrotters. Along with his younger siblings Henry and Oscar, Bailey developed his early basketball skills by shooting anything from tin cans to tar balls through the old peach basket out back. "We played with a rag ball held together by an elastic," Bailey recalls. "Except when we'd get real lucky and find an old broken tennis ball in some alley."

Oscar Robertson with his college team Cincinnati.

BIG O-LYMPIAN

The 1960 Summer Olympic Games were held in Rome, Italy. Prior to 1992, professional athletes were not allowed to compete. A recent graduate and three time All-American from the University of Cincinnati, Oscar Robertson co-captained the United States Basketball Team that year. While the team consisted of amateur athletes, it was every bit as devastating as the NBA "Dream Teams" of the 1990s.

Oscar shooting a free throw.

Along with Big O in the starting lineup were Jerry West, Walt Bellamy, Jerry Lucas, and Terry Dischinger. West, Bellamy, Lucas, and Oscar are all members of the Hall of Fame. Big O (1961), Bellamy (1962), Dischinger (1963), and Lucas (1964), all became NBA Rookies of the Year. Needless to say, they destroyed the international competition, going undefeated to bring home the Gold!

*T*RIPLE-DOUBLE SEASON

A player who in one game puts up double-digit statistics in the categories of points, assists, and rebounds, is said to have achieved a "Triple-Double." The rare feat normally occurs a handful of times each NBA season, and is usually given to great celebration.

Imagine then, a player who averages Triple-Double statistics over an entire season. That player is Oscar Robertson. During the 1961-62 season, Big O averaged 30.8 points, 11.4 assists, and 12.5 rebounds. While he very nearly accomplished this in several other seasons, it remains the only Triple-Double-Season on the NBA books!

West

A *playmaker* is rarely the biggest person on a basketball team. This common disadvantage in size is made up for with quickness and consistency. A quick first step will often fool a defender and lead to an open shot. A consistent shooter will turn this advantage into points. On defense, quickness leads to turnovers through blocked shots, steals, or loose-ball recoveries.

For 13 seasons the most consistent player in the Los Angeles Lakers' lineup was Jerry West. At slightly over six-feet, two-inches tall, he is the team's all-time leading scorer. Before statistics were kept for such things, coach Bill Sharman noted "He must have blocked three times as many [shots] as any guard in history!" Jerry remains a consistent force today as the Lakers' Executive Vice President of Basketball Operations.

Jerry Alan West is from the small town of Chelyan, West Virginia. Just up the road from Chelyan, is the town of Cabin Creek, where Jerry was born. Howard and Cecile West had six children. Jerry was next to last. Howard worked as an electrician at the local coal mine, while "Ma" looked after the household duties. The family lived in a comfortable two-story house that, according to Howard, had the "biggest front porch in town."

Jerry was six years old when his brother David began teaching him to play basketball. David was 15 at the time and was a dedicated coach for his younger sibling. Shortly before Jerry entered East Bank High School, David was drafted into the United States Army. He attained the rank of Infantry Sergeant, and died in the Korean War. His loss had a profound affect on Jerry, as he redoubled his efforts to become the best player he could be.

As a high school senior, Jerry led his basketball team to the 1956 West Virginia State High School Championship. He became the first high school player in the state's history to score 900 points in a single season. Recruiters from across the country offered scholarships hoping to lure him to their universities. Jerry's parents convinced him to attend the University of West Virginia. "I told him he belonged at home," his father said. "Home means more to a body than anything else."

Prior to 1972, college freshman were not allowed to play varsity basketball. Jerry led the West Virginia freshman team to a 17-0 record in 1957, along with regularly defeating the varsity team in practice. In his junior season, he led the Mountaineers to the final game of the NCAA Tournament, where they lost by one point (71-70) to the University of California. Despite the loss, Jerry was named the tournament's Most Outstanding Player. He completed his senior season by being named a first team All-American for the second-straight year!

The Minneapolis Lakers selected Jerry with the second overall pick in the 1960 NBA Draft. Before the season, the franchise moved to Los Angeles, California. There, Jerry joined Elgin Baylor in a lineup that reached the NBA Finals six times in the 1960s. With every appearance, came another loss at the hands of the Boston Celtics.

In 1972, the Lakers returned to the finals for the eighth time in Jerry's career. With teammate Wilt Chamberlain under the basket, Jerry set a career high for assists that season. After losing Game One to the New York Knicks, the Lakers came back to take four straight and win their first NBA Title in Los Angeles. Jerry West, one of the most consistent *playmakers* in the history of professional basketball, had become an NBA Champion at last.

PROFILE:
Jerry West
Born: May 28, 1938
Height: 6' 2"
Weight: 185 pounds
Position: Guard
College: University of West Virginia
Teams: Los Angeles Lakers (1960-1974)

CHAMPIONSHIP

SEASONS

Jerry West playing with the Lakers.

1971-72

NBA Championship
Los Angeles Lakers (4)
vs. New York Knicks (1)

EAST TO WEST

Jerry West was often regarded as a hillbilly for his small town upbringing. His Hall-of-Fame teammate Elgin Baylor liked to refer to him as "Zeke from Cabin Creek." The town of East Bank, West Virginia, annually changes its name to "West" Bank, commemorating Jerry's great high school career.

Honoring his families wishes, Jerry remained in West Virginia throughout his illustrious college career. Upon joining the NBA, he moved from his hometown of Chelyan, West Virginia (pop. 500), to one of the largest metropolitan areas in the world. Los Angeles, California, has been Jerry's home ever since. As the Lakers' all-time leading scorer, Jerry is as beloved on California's West Coast as he is revered in East Bank, West Virginia!

Jerry West playing college ball for West Virginia.

FRIEND AND FOE

Before the Lakers won the 1972 NBA Championship, Jerry West's teams made a habit of finishing second. He was named the Most Outstanding Player of the 1959 NCAA Basketball Tournament, after his Mountaineers suffered a heartbreaking loss in the final game. In 1969, Jerry was voted the MVP of the NBA Finals after suffering defeat to Bill Russell and the Boston Celtics for the sixth time.

During the 1971 season, the Los Angeles Forum hosted "Jerry West Night," in celebration of his outstanding career. Recently retired, Bill Russell arrived unannounced to honor his former rival. As he spoke, the Laker faithful fell silent out of respect for the great Celtic champion. He said: "Jerry, I once wrote that success is a journey, and that the greatest honor a man can have is the respect and friendship of his peers. You have that more than any man I know. Jerry, you are, in every sense of the word, truly a champion."

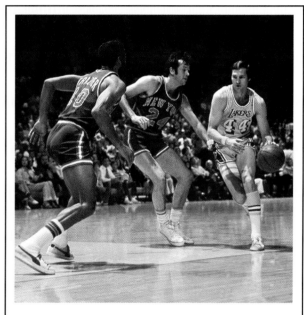

Jerry West driving to the basket.

LAKER FOR LIFE

After completing his Hall-of-Fame playing career, Jerry spent three seasons as the Lakers' head coach. Perhaps his greatest success has come as the team's general manager, as Los Angeles won five NBA Titles in the 1980s. Today, Jerry West remains a key to the Lakers' success, as the team's Executive Vice President of Basketball Operations.

Havlicek

Stamina is a quality that allows a person to keep running, long after the pain in their legs has told them to slow down. With it, a *playmaker* is able to out last a less durable opponent to gain an advantage. John Havlicek endured for 16 NBA seasons on his way to becoming the Boston Celtics' all-time leading scorer. The opposition regularly complained that "Hondo" never stopped running. Meanwhile, Boston fans were forced to endure only a handful of seasons in which John and the Celtics were *not* the league champions!

John J. Havlicek is a product of the basketball-rich Ohio River Valley. He was born in Martins Ferry, Ohio, and lived in the small town of Lansing, Ohio, just a couple of miles from the river itself. His mother Amanda, the daughter of Croatian immigrants, lived her entire life in the valley, and became John's biggest supporter. Frank Havlicek, John's father, immigrated from Czechoslovakia when he was 11 years old, and owned the local grocery store. Frank was a life long soccer fan who had trouble understanding the "American" games his son competed in. John played baseball and football

with an equal intensity to that which he brought to the basketball floor. At Bridgeport High School, he was selected for Ohio's All-State teams in all three sports. One of his closest friends in those days was Phil Niekro, who lived in the neighboring town of Blaine. Phil pursued a career in baseball, and is now listed among the greatest pitchers in Major League Baseball history. After four years of college, John would gain similar status in the NBA.

John accepted a basketball scholarship from Ohio State University in 1958. The football Buckeyes, along with teams from several other universities had also heavily recruited Hondo to play quarterback. In addition, he was invited to training camp by a number of Major League Baseball teams. John did play college baseball at Ohio State, where he became a stand-out performer. To the dismay of coach Woody Hayes, he chose not to play football.

The Buckeyes' basketball team became an immediate powerhouse when John reached varsity eligibility. He was joined on the team that season by his college roommate, Jerry Lucas. With a lineup filled with potent scorers, John put his focus on defense. Ohio State reached the NCAA Finals for three straight seasons, winning the championship in 1960. The efforts of Lucas earned him College Player of the Year honors in two straight seasons. Hondo had yet to reach his stride.

The Boston Celtics had won five of the last six NBA titles when they drafted John in 1962. Bob Cousy was entering his final season of professional basketball. Boston's entire starting lineup and part of their bench was made up of Hall-of-Fame players, making it nearly impossible for a rookie to even make the team. John played in every game that season, coming off the bench and generally running the other team to the point of exhaustion. The Celtics won six more NBA Championships in Hondo's first seven seasons! By 1970, John Havlicek was the only remaining link to the great Celtic Dynasty of the previous decade. The retirement of Bill Russell seemed to signal the end, as Boston missed the playoffs for the first time in 20 years. They returned to the post-season in 1972, and two years later the Celtics were back on top. Team captain Hondo Havlicek was still running strong. He was named the MVP of 1974 NBA Finals, and poured-in over 27 points per game throughout the playoffs.

At the age of 35, and with seven NBA championships to his credit, many wondered whether Hondo's great run had come to an end. It had not. In 1976, he was a champion once more. He retired in 1978, after playing in every game for the eighth time in his career. John made his 13th straight All-Star appearance that season, matching the record set by his former teammate, Bob Cousy. When he finally reached the finish line, Hondo the Magnificent had participated in more NBA games than any player who preceded him.

PROFILE:
John Havlicek
Born: April 8, 1940
Height: 6' 5"
Weight: 205 pounds
Position: Forward / Guard
College: Ohio State University
Teams: Boston Celtics (1962-1978)

CHAMPIONSHIP

SEASONS

1962-63
NBA Championship
Boston Celtics (4) vs. Los Angeles Lakers (2)

1963-64
NBA Championship
Boston Celtics (4) vs. San Francisco Warriors (1)

1964-65
NBA Championship
Boston Celtics (4) vs. Los Angeles Lakers (1)

1965-66
NBA Championship
Boston Celtics (4) vs. Los Angeles Lakers (3)

1967-68
NBA Championship
Boston Celtics (4) vs. Los Angeles Lakers (2)

1968-69
NBA Championship
Boston Celtics (4) vs. Los Angeles Lakers (2)

1973-74
NBA Championship
Boston Celtics (4) vs. Milwaukee Bucks (3)

1975-76
NBA Championship
Boston Celtics (4) vs. Phoenix Suns (2)

WHO'S HONDO?

John received the nickname "Hondo" in high school for his resemblance to a character played by John Wayne in a 1950s Western.

BROWN or GREEN

Even after forgoing football in college, John was drafted by the Cleveland Browns as a wide-receiver. He accepted the try out, but failed to make the final cut. He left immediately for Boston, where he became one of eight future Hall-of-Famers on the Celtics 1962-63 roster.

John Havlicek goes for the hoop.

SWING-MAN

At six-feet, five-inches tall, John Havlicek was classified as a "tweener" early in his basketball career. It was a term NBA scouts used to describe a player who was supposedly too big to play the position of guard, but too small to be a forward.

Soon, John would invent an entirely new category for himself. As a forward, he was quicker than his larger counterparts, and as a guard he out-matched his opponents with size. Playing both positions with an equal knowledge of the game's fundamentals, he became known as the NBA's original "swing-man."

Havlicek with the Celtics.

*H*ALL OF FAME CELTICS

	Position	Year of Induction	
Bob Cousy	Guard		1970
John Havlicek	Forward/Guard		1983
Thomas Heinsohn	Forward		1985
K.C. Jones	Guard		1989
Sam Jones	Guard		1983
Clyde Lovelette	Forward		1988
Frank Ramsey	Forward		1981
Bill Russell	Center		1974

Havlicek looks to pass the ball.

Walt Frazier

During the critical moments of an NBA basketball game, the *playmaker* is called upon to both inspire the defense and instigate an offensive rally. They are the ones who make the steal, block the shot, or hit the open player with a perfect pass. They perform their tasks in dramatic style and with the highest level of competency. For Walt Frazier, it was all about staying "cool" under pressure. "Clyde" was as silky smooth on the basketball court as the colorful outfits he wore off of it. In the early 1970s, he was the master of style leading the New York Knicks to a pair of NBA Championships.

Walter Frazier II was born in Atlanta, Georgia. He was the oldest of nine children. "I learned a lot about babies and changing diapers," he remembers. His father, Walter Sr., worked on an assembly line at the local automotive factory. "We weren't poor," Walt's mother, Eula Frazier, recalls. "But we weren't middle-class either. Sort of lower middle-class." At the age of nine, Walt Jr., began spending most of his time at the park near their house. On a dirt court of the ghetto playground, he learned to dribble a basketball and was soon winning most of the shooting contests he entered in with the older kids.

Walt was a star athlete of three sports at Howard High School in Atlanta. "I was always in a leadership position in all the sports I played," he said. "I was a catcher in baseball, quarterback in football, and guard in basketball. This helped me learn to be cool." His schoolmates voted Walt the Most Popular Boy in his class. He was already turning his athletic successes into a preferred life-style.

Football was Walt's favorite sport, and several colleges offered him scholarships to play. Noting that at the time there were no African-American quarterbacks in the NFL, he chose to accept a basketball scholarship from Southern Illinois University. As a sophomore, Walt led the Salukis to the NCAA Division II Championship Game, where they lost in overtime. He was named to the Little All-American Team that season, for outstanding players from small colleges.

In his senior season, SIU became the first small school to participate in the post-season National Invitation Tournament (NIT). The event is held each spring at Madison Square Garden in New York City, New York. To the surprise of everyone, the Salukis swept the competition, and Walt was named the tournament's MVP. His performance drew the attention of several NBA scouts. Walt would later say, "My whole life would be different had we not come to the NIT."

Madison Square Garden would become Walt's home court for the next 10 seasons. He was selected by the New York Knicks in the first round of the 1967 NBA Draft. That season, he was named to the league's All-Rookie Team and led the Knicks in assists. In 1970, he

combined with fellow Hall-of-Famers Dave DeBusschere, Bill Bradley, and Willis Reed to bring New York their first NBA Championship.

Walt was nicknamed "Clyde" for his stylish wardrobe, which resembled Warren Beatty's character from the hit movie "Bonnie and Clyde." He became known as the "Prince of Madison Square Garden," for the success he had brought to the Knicks. In his customized Rolls Royce, Walt became an attraction for sightseers as he glided through the streets of Manhattan. In 1972, he was joined in New York by another legendary *playmaker* with a penchant for fine cars. The next season, Earl "The Pearl" Monroe and Walt "Clyde" Frazier carried the Knicks to a second NBA Title!

PROFILE:
Walt Frazier
Born: March 29, 1945
Height: 6' 4"
Weight: 205 pounds
Position: Guard
College: University of Southern Illinois
Teams: New York Knicks (1967-1977), Cleveland Cavaliers (1977-1979)

CHAMPIONSHIP
SEASONS

Walt Frazier takes a shot.

1969-70

NBA Championship
New York Knicks (4) vs.
Los Angeles Lakers (3)

1972-73

NBA Championship
New York Knicks (4) vs.
Los Angeles Lakers (1)

DYNAMIC DUO

Earl Monroe was the 1968 NBA Rookie of the Year, and one of the greatest shooting-guards of all time. When he came to the Knicks in 1971, many fans wondered if his high profile would clash with New York's All-Star point-guard Walt Frazier. "He's 'Fire' and I'm 'Ice,'" Walt said, referring to the "Pearl's" scintillating style and his own cool demeanor.

The superstar backcourt tandem performed wonderfully together, and brought the Knick's a second NBA Title in 1973. When asked if they were the greatest guard combination in history, Clyde declared "I don't know, but I'm sure we're the only pair who ever owned Rolls Royces!"

Walt Frazier was known for his stylish dress.

WALT FRAZIER

WALT FRAZIER ENTERPRISES

Walt supported his passion for extravagant living with several successful business ventures. His popularity in the "Entertainment Capital of the World" allowed him to do commercial endorsements for products ranging from fur coats to tennis shoes. "Everything I endorse, I use," he was known to say.

In 1971, he started a business management firm and named it Walt Frazier Enterprises. "I founded the company because I knew so many guys who were losing money because of bad representation by their agents and managers," Walt said. "We handle athletes in all aspects of their daily lives including contract negotiations, investments, the paying of bills, the setting up of budgets and the securing of endorsements."

Frazier as a college player.

Walt's clients included basketball legend Julius Erving and baseball star Rusty Staub. On the basketball court, Clyde is the New York Knicks' all-time leader for Assists. Off of it, he assisted several great athletes with their financial futures.

CLYDE

In 1972, *Esquire* magazine named Walt Frazier as one of their "Best Dressed Athletes." His penthouse apartment in Manhattans's prestigious East Side neighborhood came complete with 12 closets. Clyde filled them all with his dazzling outfits, fur coats, and more than 50 pairs of shoes!

Erving

"If humans were meant to fly, they would be born with wings." The Wright brothers were among the first to prove this theory wrong, when their airplanes began taking off from the runway at Kitty Hawk, North Carolina, in the early 1900s. Sixty-some years later, America was sending Astronauts into space, while another man began to defy gravity on the courts of professional basketball. He was known as Dr. J, and his chosen course of study was in Aerial Acrobatics.

Like a human helicopter, Julius Erving would lift-off from beyond the free-throw line. Gripping the basketball as if it were a grapefruit in his claw-like hand, he would begin his ascent toward the goal. Gracefully he would glide through midair before jamming the ball through the rim with heroic force. Quite simply,

Julius could fly. In place of wings, he utilized a pair of extraordinarily powerful legs. After lifting the New York Nets to a pair of championships in the ABA (American Basketball Association), Dr. J moved his practice to the more established NBA. In the year of America's Bi-Centennial (1976), he became a member of the Philadelphia 76ers. In 1981, he became the first non-center to win the league's MVP Award since Oscar Robertson did it in 1964. Two years later, "Doc" was a champion once more.

Julius Winfield Erving II was born in Hempstead, Long Island, New York. When he was five years old his father abandoned the family of three children, and was killed by an automobile six years later. "I never really had a father," Julius said. "Then the possibility that I ever would was removed." His mother, Callie Mae, worked as a domestic servant to support the family. Soon, Julius learned to "escape" the tensions of a troubled household by playing basketball. "I'd go down to the park and play ball all day," he remembers. "It freed my head."

When Julius was 13 his mother remarried, and the family moved to Roosevelt, New York. There, Julius became a standout performer for the Roosevelt High School basketball team. "He always personified class," his high school coach recalls. His teammates took to calling him "The Doctor," for the surgical precision with which he dismantled the opposition!

Julius received a basketball scholarship from the University of Massachusetts, where he led the freshman team to an undefeated season. That year, his younger brother Marvin died of a disease later to be diagnosed as Lupus Erythematosus. "That was the most traumatic experience of my life," Julius acknowledges. "When he died, I stopped fearing—and I stopped crying." In a very short time, Dr. J would become one of the most widely acclaimed basketball stars to ever play the game.

Citing financial hardship, Julius left college after his junior season. He joined the three year old ABA, where he played first for the Virginia Squires and later with the New York Nets. In five seasons, he was selected as the league's MVP three times and averaged nearly 30 points per game. "Plenty of guys have been 'The Franchise,'" ABA Commissioner Dave Debusschere, reported. "For us, Dr. J is 'The League.'" Basketball fans spread news of his great leaping ability like folk tales since ABA games were rarely televised.

In 1976, the ABA folded, and four of its teams were merged with the NBA. The New York Nets were among the four. Struggling, however, to survive financially, they traded Julius to the Philadelphia 76ers. The legend of Dr. J continued to grow as he catapulted Philadelphia into the NBA Finals in his first season there. After suffering defeat twice more in the league championship series, the 76ers won the NBA Title in 1983. Julius Erving had proven once again, that the human race truly was meant to fly!

PROFILE:
Julius Erving
Born: February 22, 1950
Height: 6' 7"
Weight: 210 pounds
Position: Forward
College: University of Massachusetts
Teams: Virginia Squires (1971-1973), New York Nets (1973-1976), Philadelphia 76ers (1976-1987)

25

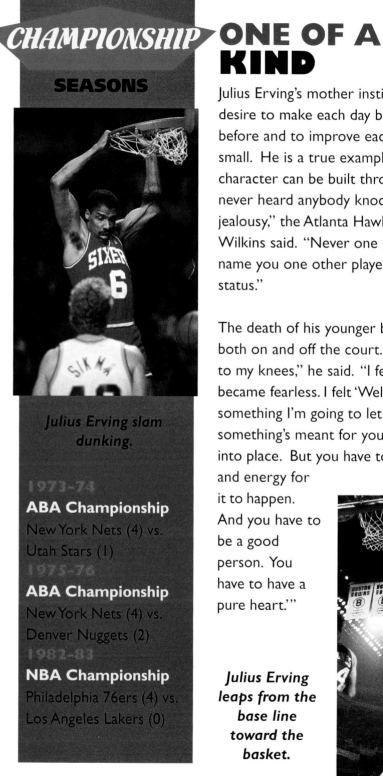

Julius Erving slam dunking.

1973-74

ABA Championship
New York Nets (4) vs. Utah Stars (1)

1975-76

ABA Championship
New York Nets (4) vs. Denver Nuggets (2)

1982-83

NBA Championship
Philadelphia 76ers (4) vs. Los Angeles Lakers (0)

ONE OF A KIND

Julius Erving's mother instilled in her children a desire to make each day better than the one before and to improve each task no matter how small. He is a true example of how human character can be built through hardship. "I've never heard anybody knock him or express jealousy," the Atlanta Hawks star Dominique Wilkins said. "Never one negative word. I can't name you one other player who has that status."

The death of his younger brother inspired Julius both on and off the court. "I was really brought to my knees," he said. "I felt helpless, but I also became fearless. I felt 'Well, if I'm going to do something I'm going to let it all hang out. If something's meant for you, then it's going to fall into place. But you have to put forth the effort and energy for it to happen. And you have to be a good person. You have to have a pure heart.'"

Julius Erving leaps from the base line toward the basket.

GOOD COMPANY

Combining his scoring totals from the ABA (11,662) and NBA (18,364), Julius Erving is one of only three professional basketball players with over 30,000 points in a career. The other two players are Kareem Abdul-Jabbar and Wilt Chamberlain.

Dr. J Flies.

SPECIAL OLYMPICS

When his professional career took flight, Julius used his financial means to support innumerable charity organizations. His charities included being National Chairman of the Hemophilia Foundation, a coach for the Special Olympics basketball program, an advisor to the March of Dimes, a spokesman for the Lupus Foundation, and an endorser of the American Red Cross. "There have been *some* better people off the court," NBA coach Pat Riley stated. "Like a few mothers and the pope. But there was only one Dr. J the player."

Bird

Legendary is a term reserved for something or someone whose greatness inspires stories that are passed down through generations. In athletics it is a status that sets a player apart from their contemporaries. It is the wizardry of a Bob Cousy assist, or Dr. J's ability to fly.

With 16 league titles to their credit, the Boston Celtics can be described as the most legendary team in the history of the NBA. In the 1980s, the Celtics' championship tradition was carried on with the most recent member of the their mythical "All-Time" lineup. Larry Bird was the self-described "Hick from French Lick." On the basketball court, he became known as "Larry Legend."

Larry Joe Bird was the fourth of six children born to Georgia and Joe Bird.

His beginnings were as simple as his name, growing-up in the small resort community of French Lick, Indiana. His father was a furniture finisher at the local piano factory, and his mother was a short-order cook and dietary consultant. Larry spent much of his childhood at the local playground watching his older brothers dominate the neighborhood basketball scene. When they were finished playing, it was Larry's turn to have the ball and he made practice part of his daily routine.

At Spring Valley High School, Larry was an outstanding pitcher for the freshman baseball team. He soon turned his full attention toward basketball. His parent's marriage was falling apart and they were divorced during Larry's junior year. One year later, his father committed suicide. Larry began spending late nights in the high school gym and back at the local playground. "I played when I was cold and my body was aching and I was so tired," he remembers. "I don't know why, I just kept playing and playing." In his senior season he was an Indiana High School All-Star, averaging over 30 points and more than 20 rebounds per game!

Larry's transition to adulthood was a bumpy ride. He was recruited by many of America's top colleges and universities, and accepted a scholarship from the University of Indiana. After less than a month away from home, he left school and returned to French Lick. He attended a local junior college for two months before dropping out to work for the city's park maintenance crew. Before his 20th birthday he was married, had a daughter, and was divorced. "I ain't no genius in school," Larry would say. "I'm a lot smarter on the court than I am in life."

When recruiters from Indiana State University came to the Bird household, Larry's mother flatly told them "He doesn't want to go to school. Leave him alone." Persistent in their course of action, they spotted him coming out of a local laundromat with his grandmother. By the end of their conversation, Larry told them "ISU may not be very good right now, but it will be when I get there!" Proving true to his word, Larry was an All-American forward in his junior season. As a senior he led the Sycamores to 33 straight wins before losing in the championship game of the 1979 NCAA Tournament. The "Hick from French Lick" was named College Player of the Year.

Larry's legendary NBA career lasted 13 seasons. The year before he arrived in Boston, the Celtics finished with their worst record since 1950. In Larry's second season, the team won its 14th NBA Championship.

By 1986, Larry had been named the league's MVP three straight times, and had turned the Celtics back into a dynasty with another pair of championship seasons. He was consistently the team's leader in scoring and defensive take-aways, and often provided the most rebounds and assists. He retired as the NBA's all-time leader for three point baskets, many of which came during critical moments to give Boston a margin of victory. Larry Bird had fulfilled his destiny. His Legend lives on.

PROFILE:
Larry Bird
Born: December 7, 1956
Height: 6' 9"
Weight: 220 pounds
Position: Forward
College: University of Indiana, Northwood Institute, Indiana State University
Teams: Boston Celtics (1979-1992)

CHAMPIONSHIP

SEASONS

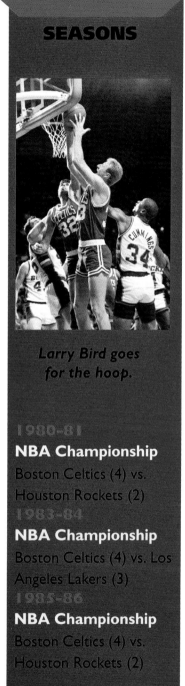

Larry Bird goes for the hoop.

1980-81

NBA Championship
Boston Celtics (4) vs. Houston Rockets (2)

1983-84

NBA Championship
Boston Celtics (4) vs. Los Angeles Lakers (3)

1985-86

NBA Championship
Boston Celtics (4) vs. Houston Rockets (2)

LEGENDARY PAIR

The Boston Celtics made Larry a first-round draft pick after his junior season. Intent on finishing his degree in Physical Education, he stayed in school. The next year he carried the Indiana State Sycamores to an undefeated season before losing to Michigan State in the NCAA Championship Game. It was the first of many classic confrontations between Larry and Earvin "Magic" Johnson.

"Until I saw Magic Johnson and Bird, I had not seen a true *playmaker* in a long time," Bob Cousy would later say. In 1980, Larry edged-out his equally legendary counterpart for Rookie of the Year honors, while Magic and the Lakers won the NBA title. Larry's Celtics and Magic's Lakers combined to win eight league titles in the decade. Each player was a three-time league MVP and they were each selected to the NBA All-Star Game 12 times. In 1992, the pair joined forces for the first time and won gold medals on the United States Olympic "Dream Team."

Larry Bird, displaying his College Player of the Year trophy.

WHAT BECOMES A LEGEND MOST?

"Larry's the best teammate a player could have." -Kevin McHale

"Bird is the best passer I've ever seen. In fact, he's so good he makes his teammates look good." -Bob Cousy

"Larry's a very unselfish player. You know if you're open you'll get the ball." -Dave Cowens

"The ultimate beauty of the kid is that he'll do anything, absolutely *anything* to win. -Red Auerbach

"Larry can very easily go out and score 30 to 35 points a game, but he's constantly aware of his teammates and what it takes to win the ballgame." -M.L. Carr

"When you combine his passing with his speed, scoring, savvy, strength, and dedication, you have to say that Larry has the potential to be the greatest all-around forward ever to play this game." -K.C. Jones

Larry Bird playing for the Celtics.

"I think it's very important that teams get along." -Larry Bird

Magic
Johnson

Once upon a time, in the fairy tale kingdom of Hollywood, there came an eminent leader. He held court in a palace known as the Great Western Forum. With a talent that bordered on the supernatural, his performances drew wide acclaim. Among the finest of his many illusions was to make a ball appear in the hands of a fellow patron at the very moment they moved to place the previously invisible object through a net.

"How does he do it?," the observers exclaimed, and exposing no sleeves he'd just smile. Only one answer would suffice to explain, it, 'twas "Magic," and so came his title.

His real name is Earvin Johnson, Jr., and he prefers *E.J.* over the nickname for which he is known worldwide. Still, from the time he was a high school all-star, "Magic" seemed to best depict his basketball prowess. He was born in Lansing, Michigan, one of 10 children in his family. His mother Christine supervised a school cafeteria, and Earvin, Sr., worked nights in the local automobile factory, hauled trash during the day, and was also a janitor. "I helped my dad on the truck, sold magazines door-to-door, shoveled peoples walks in the winter, and cut their grass in summer," Magic remembers. "I wanted to make money, to be a businessman."

From the time he was 12 years old, young Earvin could also be found shoveling snow off the basketball court at the local playground. Year-round he would practice the moves he had seen NBA players make on television. "My father would point things out to me, like Oscar [Robertson] taking a smaller guard underneath, or the pick-and-roll," he recalls. "By the time I started playing organized ball, if the coach asked whether anybody knew how to do a three-man weave or a left-handed layup, I was the first one up."

Earvin was selected for Michigan's All-State high school basketball team three straight times, and was twice named the state's Prep

Player-of-the-Year. As a senior he led Lansing Everett High School to a 27-1 record and the Class A State Championship. It was his unique ability to play every position that first earned him a reputation as a magician. His ball handling skills made him the consummate point-guard, while his great size made him a dominating center. At times it seemed as if he were playing both positions at once. When opposing teams placed multiple defenders upon him, he would confound their efforts with a pinpoint pass to an open teammate.

Michigan State University is located in the town of East Lansing, not far from the playground where Magic developed his sleight-of-hand techniques. Determined to remain a hometown hero, he accepted a scholarship there and led the Spartans to a Big Ten Conference Championship in his freshman season. As a sophomore, he was a First Team All-American, and MSU became college basketball's National Champions. The Most Outstanding Player of the 1979 NCAA Tournament was Earvin "Magic" Johnson.

When the Los Angeles Lakers made Earvin the first player selected in the 1979 NBA Draft, he packed-up his trunk and headed for the hills of Hollywood, California. His enthusiastic arrival revived a team which had not won a league title since Jerry West led the way, in 1972. Soon, the Lakers' home games would become known as "Showtime at the Fabulous Forum." Through 12 seasons and five NBA Championships, Magic was the "Master of Ceremonies."

Earvin Johnson was the tallest guard to ever play in the NBA. In 1991, he surpassed Oscar Robertson as the league's all-time leader for Assists. Before the next season, he made the shocking revelation that HIV (Human Immunodeficiency Virus) had been detected in his bloodstream. The deadly virus is the cause of the presently incurable disease known as AIDS. Though he retired at the time of the announcement, his storybook career had not quite reached the end. He returned to win a gold medal with the 1992 Olympic "Dream Team," and performed with the Lakers in 1996, before retiring for a second time.

PROFILE:
Earvin Johnson
Born: August 14, 1959
Height: 6' 9"
Weight: 255 pounds
Position: Guard
College: Michigan State University
Teams: Los Angeles Lakers (1979-1991, 1995-1996)

CHAMPIONSHIP
SEASONS

Magic Johnson.

1979-80
NBA Championship
Los Angeles Lakers (4) vs.
Philadelphia 76ers (2)
1981-82
NBA Championship
Los Angeles Lakers (4) vs.
Philadelphia 76ers (2)
1984-85
NBA Championship
Los Angeles Lakers (4) vs.
Boston Celtics (2)
1986-87
NBA Championship
Los Angeles Lakers (4) vs.
Boston Celtics (2)
1987-88
NBA Championship
Los Angeles Lakers (4) vs.
Detroit Pistons (3)

DO YOU BELIEVE IN MAGIC?

"Magic does so many incredible things on the court that you want to help him keep doing them!" -Kareem Abdul-Jabbar

"Magic sees angles a lot of guards don't see, and he gives you the ball in the rhythm of your move so you can go right up with it." -Jim Chones

"Magic is the only player who can take three shots and still dominate a game."
-Julius Erving

"I don't think Earvin will ever lose that smile. There may be times when things go wrong, but I kind of think his smile will last him his whole lifetime." -Christine Johnson

"There were just rivers of emotion coming out of him." -Jerry West

"When we're rolling and the break is going, I guess it looks like I *am* performing Magic out there." -Earvin Johnson

Magic, while playing with Michigan State.

HOCUS-POCUS

The Los Angeles Lakers won their second NBA Championship in Magic's rookie season. By the end of the 1980s, he had conjured ghosts of days gone by. The Minneapolis Lakers were the NBA's original dynasty, winning five titles in the league's first eight seasons. They were led by the incomparable center George Mikan and a Hall-of-Fame *playmaker* named Slater Martin. At five-feet, ten-inches tall, Martin could never have accomplished what Magic performed in the decisive game six of the 1980 Finals.

ONE MAN SHOW

Kareem Abdul-Jabbar was Magic's teammate for 10 seasons. With his patented "Sky Hook" the Hall-of-Fame center was the Lakers' most potent offensive weapon. In game six of the 1980 NBA Finals, however, Kareem was sidelined with a sprained ankle. The team's rookie point-guard started the game at center in place of the NBA's All-Time leading scorer.

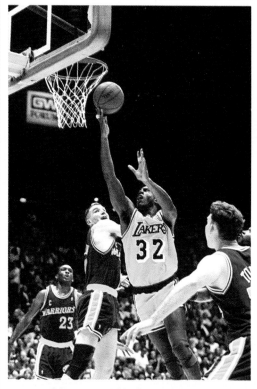

Magic with the Lakers.

By the end of the game, Magic had played every position on the floor! Leading the way he collected 42 points, with 15 rebounds, 7 assists, 3 steals, and 1 blocked shot. "Kareem brought us here," Magic proclaimed during the victory celebration of the Lakers' seventh championship. "Without the Big Fella, we wouldn't be here. We won it for him and ourselves." In the voting for the series MVP, Magic edged-out Kareem by a single vote. Later, he would develop a shot called the "Baby Hook" in honor of the elder statesman.

Isiah Thomas

The life-style of a modern NBA *playmaker* is often a glamorous one. They are the very best at what they do, and the rewards are lucrative. It is not easy to achieve such greatness, and many of the stars of professional basketball overcome long odds in order to reach the top. The tale of Isiah Thomas is one such story.

From the mean streets of Chicago's West Side ghetto, Isiah managed to rise above the trappings of poverty, which can easily swallow their unsuspecting victims. He witnessed first-hand the effects drugs, alcohol, and violence had on his neighborhood and his own family. With his family's support, however, he became a champion of both college and professional basketball. Today, Isiah is an owner and Executive Vice President of the NBA's Toronto Raptors.

Isiah Lord Thomas III was the youngest of nine children in his family. His father was a Veteran of World War II, attended trade-school and became the first African American at International Harvester to earn the position of foreman. When the plant closed down, the best job that came available to him was that of a janitor. His resentment over this fact grew into overwhelming anger, and he often reacted violently. Despairing for his own life, he left the family when Isiah was three years old.

Mary Thomas was left with nine children and without a husband. She began working at a school cafeteria, where she was allowed to bring home food for her large family. There was not always enough to go around. When neighborhood gang members showed up on the Thomas' porch, Mary met them at the door holding a double barreled shotgun. Despite many efforts to protect her children, one-by-one her sons were victimized by life on the streets. It would be left to Isiah to rescue a family on the brink of disaster.

It was soon discovered that the youngest member of the Thomas family was a basketball prodigy. At the age of three, Isiah's dribbling and shooting skills became a halftime attraction for games at a local Catholic Youth Organization. By the eighth grade he secured a scholarship at St. Joseph High School in the Chicago suburb of Westchester. The family began to pull together helping Isiah to avoid the pitfalls that had overtaken their own lives. In his senior season, he was a High School All-American and a member of his school's Academic Honor Roll.

Suddenly, Isiah's choices had grown in number. Out of the many colleges and universities who attempted recruiting him, he chose to play for Bobby Knight and the University of Indiana. "All Bobby Knight promised was he'd try to get Isiah a good education and give him a good opportunity to get better in basketball .... I liked that," Mary Thomas reported. While Isiah did not always agree with his coach's disciplinary techniques, he became an All-American in his sophomore season. Indiana won college basketball's National Championship that season, and Isiah Thomas was named the 1981 NCAA Tournament's Most Outstanding Player.

The Detroit Pistons made Isiah the second player chosen overall in the 1981 NBA Draft. Promising his mother that he would finish his college degree, he accepted a professional contract that immediately released his family from the throes of poverty. Isiah was an All-Star for 12 straight seasons, and became Detroit's all-time leader for points, assists, and steals.

The Pistons would later trade for Isiah's childhood friend Mark Aguirre, as well as Bill Laimbeer, and in 1986 they drafted a little known power-forward named Dennis Rodman. The team gained a reputation as the NBA's "Bad Boys," and in 1989 Detroit won its first NBA Championship. The following season was a repeat performance, as Isiah Thomas had completed his rise to the very top of his profession!

PROFILE:
Isiah Thomas
Born: April 30, 1961
Height: 6' 1"
Weight: 182 pounds
Position: Guard
College: University of Indiana
Teams: Detroit Pistons (1981-1994)

37

CHAMPIONSHIP

SEASONS

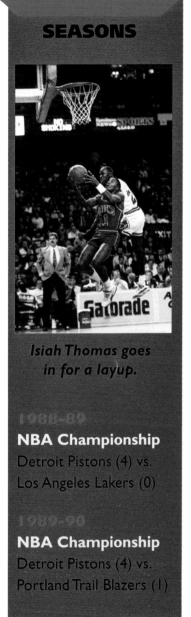

Isiah Thomas goes in for a layup.

1988-89

NBA Championship
Detroit Pistons (4) vs.
Los Angeles Lakers (0)

1989-90

NBA Championship
Detroit Pistons (4) vs.
Portland Trail Blazers (1)

SEVENTH SON

Isiah's brothers were also talented performers on the basketball court. Each found their own methods of destroying any chance they had at a pro career. When Isiah struggled to make passing grades as a high school freshman, one of his six brothers gave him some advice. "You can go one of two ways from here," he said. "I had a choice like this once. I chose hustlin'. It's a disgustin' kind of life. You got the chance of a lifetime."

His brothers would take Isiah on "field trips" to see how drug addicts and alcoholics lived in the ghetto. "From that point on," recalls his sister Ruby, "he was a changed kid." Isiah made his school's honor roll in each of the next three years.

Isiah Thomas (11) playing for Indiana.

WEST SIDE STORY

Mark Aguirre grew up eight blocks from Isiah Thomas in Chicago's gang infested West Side neighborhood known as "K-Town." "My first memory of Mark is at the Martin Luther King Boys Club," Isiah recalls. The two became regular companions on the city's playgrounds and both were named High School All-Americans.

Mark remained in Chicago attending DePaul University, while Isiah became a star for the Indiana Hoosiers.

Isiah Thomas makes a move on an opponent.

The childhood friends became starting members of the 1980 United States Olympic Basketball Team, and were first team College All-Americans in 1981. Mark was named the College Player of the Year that season, while Isiah was the Most Outstanding Player in the 1981 NCAA Tournament. In the 1981 NBA Draft, the Dallas Mavericks selected Mark with the first pick, and the Detroit Pistons took Isiah with the second selection.

In 1989, the Pistons sent Adrian Dantley to the Mavericks in return for Mark Aguirre. The West Side combo had missed their chance to compete in 1980, when the United States boycotted the Moscow Olympics. Teammates at last, Isiah and Mark brought the Detroit Pistons two straight NBA Championships!

Michael Jordan

There are people in this world who have never heard of Michael Jordan. But not many. As a professional basketball player, Michael has attained a level of recognition normally given only to world leaders, great scientists, or famous artists. Many would proclaim him as the greatest player who has ever played the game, but that alone does not explain his tremendous popularity. While it is difficult at best to designate any one person as the All-Time Greatest, there is little doubt that Michael Jordan is the most famous athlete of our time.

His name has become synonymous with basketball, and he has been likened to "Air" for the lightness with which he moves through it. Michael is not only a champion, but a phenomenon. He is an inspiration to nearly everyone he comes into contact with, and his character is nearly flawless given the scrutiny with which his life has been monitored.

When he retired from basketball after three straight NBA Championships, the Chicago Bulls dynasty was deflated. Seventeen months later Michael returned from a sojourn as a minor league baseball player to reclaim his position as the NBA's number one attraction. The Bulls have since reassumed their title as the league's premier team, while Michael's legacy continues to balloon.

Michael Jeffrey Jordan was born in Wilmington, North Carolina. He was the third son, the fourth of five children, and the only member of his family to surpass six feet in height. Delores Jordan was a supervisor at United Carolina Bank. Her husband James was an electrical engineer for General Electric. The Jordan's kept a close-knit family, and were supportive of each other's dreams. James built a regulation basketball court in the family's back yard and encouraged his children to play.

Baseball, football, and track were all sports Michael participated in as a boy, but basketball became his passion. When he was cut from the varsity team in his sophomore season at Laney High School, he was devastated. "It was all I wanted—to play on that team," Michael remembers. "It was probably good that it happened because it made me know what disappointment felt like, and I knew that I didn't want to have that feeling ever again." Before graduating, he had grown seven inches in height and led his school to the North Carolina State High School Basketball Championship.

In three seasons with the University of North Carolina Tar Heels, Michael won an NCAA Championship and was twice named basketball's College Player of the Year. He ended his freshman season by hitting a 16 foot jump shot to defeat the Georgetown Hoyas in the 1982 NCAA Final. In 1984, he co-captained the United States Olympic basketball team to a

Gold Medal at the Los Angeles games. He would win the honor a second time with the 1992 American "Dream Team," in Barcelona, Spain.

Michael has led the NBA in scoring nine times, accounting for every full season in which he has played. Before his arrival, the Chicago Bulls had won a total of 18 playoff games after 17 seasons in the league, and had never advanced to the NBA Finals. Today they are the most powerful dynasty in sports, with four NBA Titles in the 1990s, and no signs of slowing down. In 1996, Michael Jordan followed Willis Reed as only the second player in league history to be named MVP of the NBA All-Star game, regular season, and NBA Finals in the same year! Is it really any wonder he's so incredibly popular?

PROFILE:
Michael Jordan
Born: February 17, 1963
Height: 6' 6"
Weight: 216 pounds
Position: Guard
College: University of North Carolina
Teams: Chicago Bulls (1984-1993, 1994-)

41

CHAMPIONSHIP SEASONS

Michael Jordan shooting a jumper.

1990-91

NBA Championship
Chicago Bulls (4) vs. Los Angeles Lakers (1)

1991-92

NBA Championship
Chicago Bulls (4) vs. Portland Trail Blazers (2)

1992-93

NBA Championship
Chicago Bulls (4) vs. Phoenix Suns (2)

1995-96

NBA Championship
Chicago Bulls (4) vs. Seattle Supersonics (2)

THE GREATEST?

Bill Russell led the Boston Celtics to 11 NBA Championships in his 13 year career. He won the league's MVP Award five times and is considered by some to be the greatest player of all time.

Wilt Chamberlain was the NBA's MVP four times, once scored 100 points in a single game, and scored 50 or more points 118 times in his career. Some say Wilt was the best.

After Michael's sophomore season at the University of North Carolina, NBA guard Jeff Mullins speculated "The prevailing opinion always has been that Oscar Robertson and Jerry West are the two all time greatest guards. We may have to change that view because of Jordan."

In 1989, Magic Johnson confessed "Everybody talks about how it's me and Larry [Bird]—really, there's Michael, and then there's everybody else."

Outside of Chicago's United Center is a large bronze likeness of a soaring Michael Jordan. The inscription below proclaims:"The best there ever was. The best there ever will be." It is an opinion shared by many.

Jordan makes a move.

"AIR" TIME

1979- Sophomore Michael Jordan fails to make the varsity basketball team at Wilmington, North Carolina's Laney High School

1981- Named MVP of the Laney High School basketball team and leads them to the North Carolina State High School Championship

1982- Sinks a last second basket to give the University of North Carolina the NCAA Championship

1983- Wins the first of two straight College Player of the Year Awards

1984- Leads United States team to an Olympic Gold Medal

1985- NBA Rookie of the Year

1986- Plays only 18 games due to injury

1987- Wins the first of two straight NBA Slam Dunk Championships at All-Star break

1988- Named MVP of both the All-Star game and NBA regular season, and wins Defensive Player of the Year Award

1991- Named MVP of both NBA regular season and NBA Finals

1992- Named MVP of both NBA regular season and NBA Finals, wins his second Olympic Gold Medal with the United States "Dream Team"

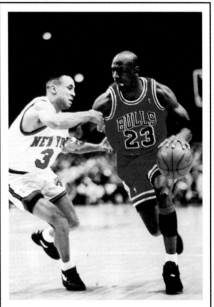

Jordan driving to the hoop.

1993- After setting an NBA Finals record for average points per game (41.0), Michael is named the MVP of the league's championship series for the third straight time

1994- After retiring from the NBA, Michael signs a contract with the Chicago White Sox and plays minor-league baseball for the Birmingham Barons

1995- Michael returns to the NBA

1996- Chicago Bulls finish with the best record in league history (72-10), Michael is named MVP of the All-Star game, regular season, and the NBA Finals!

Glossary

All-American: A person chosen as the best amateur athlete at their position.

Assist: A pass of a basketball that enables a teammate to score.

Contract: A written agreement a player signs when they are hired by a professional team.

Dunk: To slam a ball through the basket from above.

Field Goal: In basketball, a converted shot worth either two or three points.

Final Four: The name given to the last four teams remaining in the NCAA college basketball championship tournament.

Foul: Illegal contact with another player. Basketball players are allowed a limited amount of fouls per game (usually five or six).

Foul Out: To be put out of a game for exceeding the number of permissible fouls.

Free Throw: A shot taken while the game clock is stopped as a result of a foul by the opposing team, worth one point and taken from the free throw line.

Freshman: A student in the first year of a U.S. high school or college.

Junior: A student in the third year of a U.S. high school or college.

NCAA: An organization that oversees the administration of college athletics (National Collegiate Athletic Association).

NBA: An organization of professional basketball teams in North America (National Basketball Association).

Rebound: To retrieve and gain possession of the ball as it bounces off the backboard or rim after an unsuccessful shot.

Scholarship: A grant given to a student to pay for their college tuition.

Senior: A student in the fourth year of a U.S. high school or college.

Sophomore: A student in the second year of a U.S. high school or college.

Statistics: Numbers used to estimate a player's ability in different categories.

Varsity: The principal team representing a university, college, or school in sports, games, or other competitions.

Index

Symbols

1960 Summer Olympics 11

A

Abdul-Jabbar, Kareem 9, 27, 34, 35,
Aguirre, Mark 37, 39
American Basketball association 24
assists 5, 8, 9, 11, 13, 21, 29, 35, 37
Atlanta Hawks 6, 26
Auerbach, Red 7, 31

B

Baylor, Elgin 13, 14
Big "O" 8, 9, 11
Big Ten Conference 33
Boston Celtics 4, 5, 6, 7, 13,
    15, 16, 17, 18, 28, 29, 30,
    34, 42
Boston College 7

C

Chamberlin, Wilt 13, 27, 42
Chicago Bulls 40, 41, 42, 43
Chicago Stags 6
Cinncinnati Reds 5, 7, 9
College of the Holy Cross 5
College Player of the Year 9, 17, 29,
    41, 43
Cousy, Bob 4, 5, 6, 7, 17, 19, 28, 30,
    31
Cowens, Dave 31

D

DeBusschere, Dave 21, 25
De Paul University 39
Detroit Pistons 34, 37, 38, 39
Dr J 24, 25, 27, 28
Dream Team 11, 30, 33, 41, 43

E

Erving, Julius 23, 24, 25, 26, 27, 34

F

Frazier, Walt 20, 21, 22, 23
French Lick, Indiana 28

G

Georgetown Hoyas 41
Great Wetern Forum 32

H

Harlem Globetrotters 10
Havlicek, John 16, 17, 19
Hayes, Woody 17
Hondo 4, 16, 17, 18
Houdini of the Hardwood 4, 5

I

Indiana State Sycamores 30
Indiana State University 29

J

Johnson, Earvin 32, 33, 34
Johnson, Magic 30, 42
Jones, K.C. 19, 31
Jordan, Michael 40, 41, 42, 43

K

Knight, Bobby 37

L

Laimbeer, Bill 37
Los Angeles Lakers 6, 12, 13, 14, 18, 22, 26, 30, 33, 34, 35, 38, 42
Lucas, Jerry 11, 17

M

Madison Square Garden 21
McHale, Kevin 31
Michigan State University 33
Mikan, George 6, 10, 14, 18, 35
Milwaukee Bucks 8, 9, 10, 18
Minneapolis Lakers 6, 13, 18, 35
Monroe, Earl 22

N

Naismith Memorial Basketball Hall of Fame 5
National Basketball Association 4
National Invitation Tournament 21
NBA All Star 4, 30, 41
NBA All Star Game 30, 41
NBA Draft 6, 13, 21, 33, 37, 39
NBA's Rookie of the Year 9
NCAA Division 11, 21
NCAA Finals 17
NCAA Tournament 13, 29, 33, 37, 39
New York City 4, 5, 21

New York Knicks 13, 14, 20, 21, 22, 23
New York Nets 24, 25, 26

O

Ohio State University 16, 17

P

Philadelphia 76ers 24, 25, 26, 34
point guard 4, 5, 7, 22, 33, 35

R

rebounds 8, 11, 28, 29, 35
Reed, Willis 21, 41
Riley, Pat 27
Robertson, Oscar 7, 8, 9, 11, 24, 33, 42
Rodman, Dennis 37
Russell, Bill 5, 7, 15, 17, 19, 42

S

Southern Illinois University 21

T

Thomas, Isiah 36, 37, 39
Toronto Raptors 36
Tri-Cities Blackhawks 6
Triple-Double 11

U

UCLA 9
United States Army 12
University of Cinncinnati 9, 11
University of Indiana 29, 37
University of Massachusetts 25
University of North Carolina 13
University of West Virginia 13

V

Virginia Squires 25

W

West, Jerry 11, 12, 13, 14, 15, 33, 34,
    42
Wilkins, Dominique 26